THANKSGIVING DAY THANKS

By Laura Malone Elliott

Illustrated by Lynn Munsinger

KT KATHERINE TEGEN BOOKS
An Imprint of HarperCollins Publishers

Also by Laura Malone Elliott and Lynn Munsinger

A String of Hearts
Hunter's Best Friend at School
Hunter and Stripe and the Soccer Showdown
Hunter's Big Sister

Katherine Tegen Books is an imprint of HarperCollins Publishers.

Thanksgiving Day Thanks
Text copyright © 2013 by Laura Malone Elliott
Illustrations copyright © 2013 by Lynn Munsinger
All rights reserved. Manufactured in China.
No part of this book may be used or reproduced in any manner whatsoever without
written permission except in the case of brief quotations embodied in critical articles
and reviews. For information address HarperCollins Children's Books, a division of
HarperCollins Publishers, 10 East 53rd Street, New York, NY 10022.
www.harpercollinschildrens.com

Library of Congress Cataloging-in-Publication Data is available.
ISBN 978-0-06-000236-7

The artist used watercolor, pen and ink, and pencils on Waterford
Saunders watercolor paper to create the illustrations for this book.
Typography by Rachel Zegar
13 14 15 16 17 SCP 10 9 8 7 6 5 4 3 2 1
❖
First Edition

For Aunt Ann,
who hosted Thanksgiving dinner when I was young
and always makes family time special
—L.M.E.

Thanksgiving is coming," said Sam's teacher, Mrs. Wright. "What one special thing about the holiday would you give thanks for?"

"Football!" shouted Nicole.

"Sweet potatoes with marshmallows!" Jeffrey yelled.

"Shopping!" announced Tiffany.

Sam wasn't sure what his one special thing would be.

"Who knows the story of the very first Thanksgiving?" asked Mrs. Wright.

Sam's best friend, Mary Ann, knew. "When the Pilgrims came to America, Native Americans showed them how to plant corn and hunt for food. So the Pilgrims invited the Native Americans to a big feast to celebrate their friendship and their first harvest."

"That's right," said Mrs. Wright. "How should we celebrate Thanksgiving in class?"

"We can have our own feast," Jeffrey suggested.

"We can dress up like Pilgrims and Native Americans," said Mary Ann.

"Oh, goodee!" Tiffany clapped her hands. "Costumes!"

Sam didn't have any ideas. He was stuck on figuring out what he was thankful for.

Winston's hand shot up. "My grandmother makes a turkey out of yarn for Thanksgiving."

"Eeeeew," squealed Tiffany. "You eat yarn turkey?"

"Eeeeew!" squealed her friends.

"No, it's a decoration," Winston said. "Before dinner, we write what we are thankful for on a paper feather and stick it in the turkey."

"That's a great tradition," said Mrs. Wright. "Everyone pick one thing you are really thankful for to write on a feather. And I don't mean candy," she added with a smile.

Uh-oh, thought Sam.

The class came up with all sorts of Thanksgiving projects.
Jeffrey organized a pumpkin-pie-making contest.

Nicole made special place mats. She collected red
and orange maple leaves and pressed them between
two sheets of wax paper.

While shopping for a Pilgrim outfit, Tiffany learned about a Thanksgiving food drive for the needy and donated cans of soup.

Winston built a miniature *Mayflower*, just like the Pilgrims' ship, from Popsicle sticks.

Mary Ann made a headband out of white and purple beads to look like the wampum of the Wampanoag tribe.

She also practiced with a bow and arrow until each arrow's rubber-suction head stuck to the target's bull's-eye.

Meanwhile, Sam worried.

"*Wuneekeesuq.*" Mary Ann tried to cheer him up.

"That's how the Wampanoag say 'Good day.'"

Usually Sam liked to learn the big words Mary Ann used. But not this time. "There's nothing good about it—I still haven't figured out my project." Sam sighed. "Or what I'm thankful for."

"Think about what you enjoy most on Thanksgiving Day," Mary Ann suggested.

Sam thought and thought.

The day of the feast arrived. Tables were heaped
with food and autumn decorations.

Jeffrey had dressed up as Governor Bradford. Tiffany was Priscilla from Longfellow's poem about pilgrims. Mary Ann was Squanto.

"Where's your project?" Mary Ann asked Sam.

"It's outside. It's a surprise."

The class lined up to write their thanks on the paper turkey feathers.

Jeffrey was thankful for turkey stuffing.

Winston was thankful for the school janitor being so nice about his flooding the cafeteria when testing his *Mayflower*.

Mary Ann was thankful for books.

It was almost Sam's turn.

All of a sudden, a HUGE gust of wind rattled the classroom windows. A storm was coming. "Oh no!" Sam cried. "My project!"

Sam dashed outside to a tree to untie his surprise—
a bunch of enormous balloons!

He fought his way back through the wind toward the classroom, sticking close to the school building.

Everyone darted to the window just in time to see a big dog bobbing by! Then a cat popped up! And a turkey, and a frog. It was just like the Thanksgiving Day parade on TV!

Another blast of wind whipped the balloons.
The frog popped. The turkey broke loose. The cat
flew away.

"Oh dear," said Mrs. Wright.

Mary Ann grabbed her bow and arrows.
And the yarn turkey. She raced outside.

Sam was chasing the dog, its string just out of his reach. Mary Ann tied the turkey's yarn to an arrow. She took aim. *Ziiiiinnnngggg.* The arrow's rubber cup stuck to the dog's long nose. Mary Ann reeled in.

"YAY!" cheered the students.

But Sam was sad. "I can't have a parade with only
one balloon," he said. "And I still don't know what to
write on my feather."

Mary Ann thought for a minute. "Your parade was
a great idea, Sam. Is there something about the big
Thanksgiving Day parade you're thankful for?"

"Well, my whole family watches it together. We drink hot chocolate and tell stories. Grandpop talks about going to New York City for the parade when he was little. We laugh a lot." Sam smiled. Now he knew what to put on his feather.

Later Sam wrote another feather and tucked it into Mary Ann's headband.

A Note About Thanksgiving

Seeking a better life in the New World, the Pilgrims braved a stormy Atlantic Ocean in the tiny *Mayflower.* (Its perimeter was just a little bigger than a tennis court's.) Once they landed in what is now Massachusetts, the Pilgrims faced many hardships. They probably would not have survived without the help of the Wampanoag tribe and Squanto, a Pawtuxet Native American who had learned English while a captive of English explorers.

Squanto taught the Pilgrims to grow corn, beans, and squash (vegetables the Native Americans called the "three sisters"). He showed them how to tap maple trees for syrup and where to gather shellfish such as clams. He convinced the Wampanoag to be friends with the Pilgrims.

In 1621, grateful they had food for the winter, Governor William Bradford called for a day of thanksgiving. Such celebrations were a harvest tradition in England. He invited the Wampanoag. The feast was very different from today's. Although wild turkey was probably on the menu (along with eel and swan meat), pumpkin pies, cranberry sauce, and sweet potatoes definitely were not. Instead, the Pilgrims might have enjoyed succotash—a stew of corn and lima beans—or pemmican—crushed cranberries and dried deer meat in melted fat.

Other Thanksgiving Facts

• President Lincoln called for a national day of thanksgiving in October 1863 during the Civil War, but Congress did not make it an official national holiday until 1941.

• Macy's Thanksgiving Day Parade started in 1924. Children's book illustrator Tony Sarg created its first hot-air balloon. Snoopy has been in the parade more than any other balloon character.

• The tradition of playing football games on Thanksgiving started with college championship matches in the 1890s.

• The idea that Thanksgiving weekend should be the kickoff for the Christmas shopping season was started by President Franklin D. Roosevelt to help shopkeepers during the Depression.

• One of the largest pumpkin pies ever made weighed 2,020 pounds and had 1,860 eggs and 300 pounds of sugar in it.

• Minnesota is the top turkey-producing state.

• A ripe cranberry can bounce.